CONTENTS

chapter
ONE

P.I. OR Pee-yew?

🐾

"Pee-yew!" Ziggy Fluffenscruff barked. "This case stinks!"

The Pup Investigators Pack almost always found themselves in strange spots while solving crimes, but this was their first time in a sewer. They were on the hunt for a stolen wheel of rare aged cheese called the Big Cheddar.

"Keep sniffing for the cheesy trail," Rider Woofson said. He was the leader of the P.I. Pack and the best dog detective in Pawston.

"*Bow-wowza!* I'm trying. But all I smell is . . . yuck!" the pup said. Ziggy was the youngest member

of the Pack, but he had a nose for finding clues.

"Hey, Westie, shine your light this way," said Rora Gooddog. She had a sharp eye for details, even in the dim, dirty sewer.

"Sure thing," Westie Barker said.

He pointed a giant helmet flash-light toward Rora. The flashlight was his latest invention, and it was a bright idea in the darkness of the tunnel.

"More crumbs," Rora said. "Looks like whoever stole the Big Cheddar stopped for a snack. They left us an actual trail of bread crumbs."

"Ugh," Ziggy said with watery eyes. "I can't believe I'm saying this, but I think I've lost my appetite. That's how bad it stinks down in this place."

"Hang in there, Ziggy," Rider said. "These sewer lines run right under the Chinchilla Cheese Shop. It's the perfect escape route

for an underground crook."

"Who would come this way?" Ziggy asked. "It smells worse than a locker full of old dirty socks."

Rider stopped to examine some footprints. "I smell a rat . . . a sewer rat."

"Hey, that's offensive!" said rats from the floor and pipes above. "Just because we live down here don't mean we're thieves!"

"Then you won't mind telling us where you were between the hours of midnight and two a.m. this morning," Rider said.

Before the rats could answer, a loud cry echoed in the tunnel. The P.I. Pack and the gang of rats followed the sound.

Standing around a bend in the tunnel was a handsome and heroic-looking husky. He was handcuffing a large alligator.

"Hey! You've got the wrong lady, Detective!" the reptile cried.

"I don't think so, Allie Gator," the husky said. "Shame on you for stealing the Big Cheddar. You should have known better than to try to frame those innocent sewer rats with me in town."

"What are you talking about?" Allie cried. "What's a 'big cheddar'? And who are you?!"

"I'm Detective Wolf Growler," the husky said. "And you have the right to remain silent."

"Hold on," Rider said. "What proof do you have? Did you find the

Big Cheddar on Ms. Gator? I think the rats are the culprits."

"I'm afraid you've been fooled," Growler said as he motioned toward Allie Gator. "This reptile made it look like the rats were guilty. Did you notice that the crumb trail was scattered too far apart to have been left by rats? Rats are short and take smaller steps, but gators are

tall. They take bigger steps and leave crumbs farther apart."

How did I not notice that? Rider wondered.

As Rider watched the husky escort Allie Gator to jail, he saw that his teammates were dazzled by Wolf Growler's slick detective work. Could it be that Rider Woofson had finally met his match? Was Wolf Growler the new super-detective in town?!

chapter
TWO

DOG INSTINCT

🐾

The next day, Rider arrived at the P.I. Pack office later than usual. Ziggy hid his nose under his paws. "*Bow-wowza*, Boss. You stink!"

"But I washed twice last night," Rider said.

"Don't feel bad," Westie said. "He says we all stink. I know for a fact that I smell as fresh as a daisy. I went to the groomers and had a major sham*poodle* after our trip to the sewer. Ziggy's nose is just too strong for its own good."

"It's true!" Ziggy whimpered. "I took four baths, and I still can't shake the stench."

Ziggy sprayed himself with air freshener, hoping to chase the smell away.

"Rider, how are you? Is everything okay?" Rora asked.

"You're never late to the office."

"I stopped by the police station to talk to Allie Gator," Rider said. "Something about this case smells all wrong."

"You're telling me!" Ziggy moaned as he pulled out some soap and scrubbed his head.

"Here's what I found out. First, the Big Cheddar is still missing. And second, Allie Gator is allergic to cheese," Rider said.

He scribbled the facts in his notepad.

"That could be a load of *croc*," Rora suggested. "Maybe Allie stole the Big Cheddar and hid it to sell to the highest bidder."

"Yes, and let's not forget that

Detective Growler was right about the crumbs yesterday," added Westie as he worked on a new invention. "I was very impressed with his detective skills."

Ziggy was covered in bubbles now. "Also, if it weren't for Growler, we would still be down in that smelly sewer chasing our tails."

"Still, it doesn't feel right," Rider said.

"Don't be jealous, Boss," Rora said. "You can't be the one who solves every case."

Rider felt hurt. He knew his P.I. Pack teammates were his friends, but he could also see how much

they liked Wolf Growler. Maybe Rora was right—maybe he really *was* jealous of this new detective. Maybe his feelings were clouding his judgment.

Still, Rider had always trusted his instincts, and his gut said there was more to this mystery.

The phone rang, and Rider answered it. "Hello. What's that, Mr. Mayor? There's been another robbery? This time at the Museum of Feline Art! We're on our way."

DIS-ARMED AND DANGEROUS

When the P.I. Pack arrived at the museum, there was already another husky sleuth on the scene.

"Mr. Mayor, I thought you wanted me on this case?" Rider asked.

"Huh? Oh! You mean Wolf Growler." The mayor waved over the other detective. "Yes, I have

asked you both here today. This is the first robbery at the Museum of Feline Art, and the owner has his tail in a tizzy. An ancient two-thousand-year-old statue of CleoCatra has had its arms stolen."

"Why would someone only steal a statue's arms?" Rora asked.

"We don't know," the mayor said. "That is why I need the best of the best working together on this case."

"Mr. Mayor, my P.I. Pack and I have been working in Pawston for years. No one knows these streets and these citizens like we do. However, if you think it best, then we're happy to work with Mr. Growler." Rider extended his

paw to the new detective for a friendly handshake.

Growler took one look at Rider and snorted. "No, thanks. I prefer to work alone. Besides, I've already gathered enough evidence to solve this case by tonight."

"But you just got here," the mayor said.

"I know. I'm *that* good," Growler bragged as he left the museum.

Rider turned his attention to the scene of the crime. He searched the room, looking for any clues that Growler might have missed.

He had to prove he was still the best detective in Pawston.

"So, Mr. Mayor, what's the story on this not-so-humble husky?" asked Rora.

"Detective Growler has only been in town a few weeks," said the mayor. "He's already solved several small cases, and he solved

them faster than any detective I've ever known . . . including, um, Rider."

"Speed isn't everything," Westie said. "Sometimes working slower is working smarter."

"Not in thissss city," Mr. Meow said when he walked into the room. He was one of the richest— and rudest—cats in town. He was also good friends with the owner of the museum.

"If you're not fasssst enough, you might get left behind."

"Sometimes that's a good place to be," Rider said from behind a giant statue of a Roman emperor named Catius Clawdius. He'd found another trail of crumbs just like he had seen in the sewer

the day before. Next to them, he'd found a set of tiny tools hidden in the shadows. They were the perfect size to be used by rats.

Before Rider could tell everyone about his discovery, the police radios went crazy and the mayor's cell phone rang. "What?! There's been *another* robbery! This time at the Pawston Library."

BOOKS AND BOOKED

The P.I. Pack arrived at the library
to find the head librarian in tears.
Mr. Paul R. Bear was blowing his
nose into a handkerchief as Rider
approached. "Hello, sir. Could you
tell me what happened?"

"I was away at lunch when my
assistant called me," Mr. Bear
sniffled. "Our rare-book room was

broken into. Pawston Library is home to some of the oldest books in the country. It was my job to keep them safe and . . . and . . ." He burst into blubbery tears again.

"Do you know how many books were stolen?" Rora asked gently.

"Just one," said the librarian. "It was a cookbook that was more than three hundred years old."

Mr. Bear brought the P.I. Pack into the rare-book room, but someone was already there. "Hey, what are you doing?" asked the librarian.

Wolf Growler was dusting for paw prints. "My job," the detective said with a smirk. "Now, if you don't mind moving out of my way, I can find the crook who stole your cookbook."

"I don't mean to tell you how to do your job, Growler, but in Pawston, we are nice to one another," said Rora.

"I don't have time to be nice," Growler growled. "I have a crime to solve. And it looks like I just did."

Growler pointed to the paw prints all over the scene of the crime. He pulled out a small computer and began to scan the prints.

"All I have to do is run these prints through the police database, and I'll have my criminal in no time at all."

Rider patted Mr. Paul R. Bear's back as he continued to sob while Rora looked around. The first thing she noticed was that a small air vent had been left open.  Before she could examine the clue, Growler cleared his throat.

"Ahem. Well, well, well . . .

what do we have here?" The husky
grinned and grabbed Ziggy by the
back of his collar. "Looks like you
just couldn't stay away."

"Huh?!" Ziggy yipped.

"Let go of my teammate at
once," Rider barked.

"No can do, Detective," Growler said. "It looks like I've *collared* my criminal mastermind."

"Ziggy?" Rora laughed. "He's not a mastermind of anything. No offense, kid."

"None taken," Ziggy said.

"What are you talking about, Growler?" demanded Rider.

"Your friend's paw prints are all over the cookbook shelves. That's what we call proof," Growler said.

"Plus everyone knows about this pup's unstoppable hunger. That's what we call motive."

"Having a bottomless stomach doesn't make him a criminal," Rider said.

"That's right. Neither does enjoying the public library," Westie added. "Ziggy and I come here every Saturday. He reads cookbooks while I look at science manuals. I'd hardly call that a crime."

"I'd hardly call it an accident, either," Growler said. "So now I'm taking Mr. Ziggy Fluffenscruff to the police station to be booked and questioned."

"Don't worry, Zig," Rider said. "I'll figure this out."

"I bet you will," Growler said with a sneer. "After all, the bad apple doesn't fall far from the tree."

"And what is that supposed to mean?" Rora demanded.

"It means," Growler explained, "that I wouldn't be surprised if Rider was mixed up in all these crimes too."

chapter
FIVE

BLAMED AND FRAMED

Detective Wolf Growler and several police officers led Ziggy to their patrol car—in handcuffs. Rider had never seen the young pup look so sad and scared.

"I didn't do it! I swear on my mother's lasagna!" Ziggy cried before they closed the door.

"He's innocent," said Westie.

"I know," Rider agreed. "Now we need to figure out who the real crook is to save our friend." He rushed over to the librarian. "The cookbook that was stolen—what kind of recipes did it have?"

"Fondue recipes," he said.

"Well, Ziggy is fond of recipes,"

Westie said. "He loves food."

"Not 'fond of,'" Rora explained. "*Fondue.* It's a dish prepared by melting cheese and dipping food into it."

"Have any suspicious or strange characters been hanging out near the cookbook shelf this week?" Rider asked.

"Hmmm . . . ," the librarian thought. "There was a suspicious snake in a trench coat and a hat here this morning."

"How is that suspicious?" Rora asked, looking over at Rider, who wore a trench coat and a hat.

"Well, he was a snake, but he didn't slither," said the librarian. "He crawled."

"Oh! I have just the invention to help us!" Westie cried. He pulled out a strange device covered in wires and bulbs. "I call it the Bust-Duster 3000. It blasts out dust that clings to every animal print in the room."

Westie pushed a button, and *POOF!* A white cloud exploded, coating everything in powder.

"Thanks for that, bonehead," Rora said with a cough.

"Look!" Rider said, pointing at the floor. "There's not a snake track in sight, but there is a line of small footprints followed by little tail marks. They lead right to the stolen book's bookcase. Judging by the size and movement of the prints, I'd say we're dealing with rats."

"This is odd," said Westie. He was looking at the paw prints Growler said belonged to Ziggy. "These aren't dog prints at all. They are cat prints!"

"Hmm . . . cats and rats? Working together?" Rora questioned. "That's not a good sign."

"I think someone is treating Ziggy like a picture," said Rider. "He's been framed."

chapter
SIX

A CHEESY CHASE

🐾

Rora, Westie, and Rider left the library more determined than ever. "We have to save Ziggy," Westie said. "Where should we start?"

"First we need to find the Big Cheddar," Rider said. "Then I bet we'll find the real crooks."

Crossing the street at that

very moment was a familiar face: the criminal henchdog Rotten Ruffhouse. He was carrying a giant wheel of cheese.

"Well, someone get a camera and say cheese," Rora said. "Rotten's got the Big Cheddar!"

"Don't move a paw, scoundrel!" Rider shouted.

"Oh no! Of all the rotten luck!" the rottweiler yelped as he took off running. He darted into the crowded street and dodged between the cars. The cheesy chase was on!

Rider and Rora followed Rotten

through the streets while Westie
took to the air with another of his
inventions—a Helicop-T-shirt!

"He's turning left onto Bark Avenue!" Westie shouted from above.

Rider and Rora leaped over carts as they chased Rotten into the Pawston shopping district.

They burst into a grooming salon,
where animals were having their
fur washed, dyed, and trimmed.
As the three of them bounded over
customers, the barbers were having all sorts of close shaves!

"This is getting hairy!" yelled Rider as the chase led them back outside.

Next the thief ran into the Tarantula Tea Shop with the detectives in hot pursuit.

BANG! CRASH! SPLASH!

The dainty spider-
web tables were not
built to withstand
such a ruckus. Teacups and
kettles fell left and right as the
dogs whisked past fancy spiders,
who fainted with surprise.

Then Rotten rocketed into the

Little Kiddie Yarn Barn, an indoor playground. Kittens were everywhere, cuddling with soft, colorful balls of yarn. Rider and Rora slowed down to carefully step over the little ones, but the frisky kittens thought it was a game. They batted their strings and made a net that trapped the two detectives.

"Looks like you're all tied up!" said Rotten as he escaped out the back door.

Westie landed one minute too late. "I'm sorry, Rider. I lost him."

"So did we, Westie," Rider said as he pulled off the strings and the happy little kittens. "But it wasn't a complete loss."

"It wasn't?" Rora asked. "The crook and the Big Cheddar got away!"

"Now we know a few things . . . ," Rider began. "We know that Rotten Ruffhouse is involved. We also

know that Rotten is working with someone else. He always does. Lastly, and most importantly, we know why they needed Ziggy arrested."

"Why?" Westie asked.

"Because of Ziggy's super-nose," Rora said. "The kid would have sniffed out the Big Cheddar in no time."

"Exactly," Rider agreed. "We are going to need Ziggy's help."

"But he's in jail," Westie said.

"Not for long," Rider said with a wink.

chapter SEVEN

PAWSTON POUND

A PRISON (SNACK) BREAK

"Rider, you cannot really be considering this!" Westie said as the P.I. Pack van pulled up outside the Pawston Pound.

"I most certainly am," Rider said. He handed black suits and masks to his teammates. "We all know Ziggy is innocent, but we need his help to prove it. That means breaking him out of the pound."

"How are we going to do that?" Rora asked. "There are guards everywhere."

"We're going to walk in the front door," Rider said. "Good thing we know a pup on the inside."

"We do?" Westie asked.

"We do." Rider pointed. Sitting at the front desk watching TV was Frenchie, the nice

but bumbling French bulldog.

The P.I. Pack watched from the van until Frenchie fell asleep a few minutes into his night shift. "Time to go," Rider said, pulling on his disguise.

Dressed in all black, the three dog detectives slinked along the shadows and then tiptoed in through the front door. Quickly and quietly, they moved like cats until they found their friend sleeping in his cage.

"Ziggy, wake up!" whispered Rider.

Ziggy stirred awake and rubbed his eyes. "Rider? Is that you, or is this a dream?" he whispered. "Did you bring any snacks? The food is terrible in here."

"Same old Ziggy,"
Rora said as she
reached for the
door.

"Wait! If you
open this door, the
alarm will go off,"
Ziggy warned. "You
should go before you
get caught."

"We're not leaving without you,"
Rider said. "Westie, Phase One."

Westie pulled out an oversize
magnet. "Stand back, Ziggy. My
Magno-Bender will bend those bars!"

Bzzzzzzz!

A moment later, Ziggy was free. His tail wagged as he hugged his friends. "Thanks, guys, but for real, do you have any snacks? I'm starving."

"Rora, Phase Two," Rider said.

"You'll like this one, kid," Rora told Ziggy. She pulled out a round ball of fur and placed it in Ziggy's cell. Then she pressed a button, and the ball inflated like a balloon until it was the same size as Ziggy. Rora put it on the cot and covered it with a blanket. "Now no one will notice you're missing."

"That's brilliant!" Ziggy said.

"All right, Westie," said Rider. "Bend the bars back, and let's

get out of here. We have a cheesy crime to solve."

The four friends hurried back the way they'd come. Frenchie was still sound asleep and snoring

at the front desk. Once they were in the van, all of the P.I. Pack breathed a deep sigh of relief.

"I can't believe we actually pulled it off!" Westie said.

"Only thanks to your invention and Rora's smarts," Rider said.

"It's good to have you back, Ziggy," Rora said.

"It would be better if you'd brought me some snacks," Ziggy whimpered as his tummy gurgled loudly.

"Well, let's start looking for one," Rider said. "I hope you're in the mood for cheese."

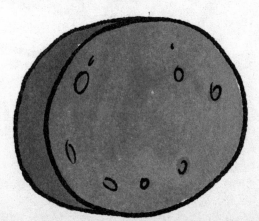

chapter
EIGHT

FONDUE FACTORY

🐾

"Uh-uh! No way!" Ziggy complained from the back of the van. "I am not going back into the sewer!"

"Luckily, we don't have to," Rider said. "The last place we saw the Big Cheddar was on Bark Avenue. We can't sniff out the trail, but you can."

The P.I. Pack drove to the back

of the Little Kiddie Yarn Barn. Ziggy's nose picked up the scent instantly. "Mmmm, this delicious cheddar reminds me of nachos," Ziggy said as he drooled a little. "Any chance I can eat the Big Cheddar when we find it?"

"How many times have we told

you, kid," Rora said, "you can't eat the evidence?"

Ziggy's stomach grumbled as the young pup started giving directions. He hung his head out the window, letting his fur fly back and his tongue lap in the wind.

After a while, Ziggy said, "Take a right here. The yummy smell is stronger than ever. We're close!"

They had arrived at an old warehouse outside the city. The P.I. Pack parked, changed outfits, and snuck up the fire escape. Once they were on the roof, they peeked through an open skylight window.

"Are those rats?" Westie asked.

"They are," Rora said. "Rats in cooking hats, cooking in vats.

Talk about a tongue twister."

Down below were dozens of
rats—including the sewer rats
Rider had questioned before Wolf
Growler arrested Allie Gator. They

were all wearing white chef's hats. Some were cutting up blocks of cheese. Others were slicing giant loaves of bread, and some were standing over the large vats, stirring the melting cheese.

The head rat chef was in the center of the room. He was reading the stolen book of fondue recipes from the library. Next to him was another chef holding the missing

arms of CleoCatra. He was using the arms to stir the cheese.

"It's a fondue factory!" Ziggy said. "I must be in cheddar heaven. You don't mind if I sneak down and have a little bite, do you?"

"Keep your eyes on the prize, Zig," Rider said. "We need to catch the real crooks so you don't go back to jail."

"Oh, that's right." Ziggy frowned. "Well, let's get down there and arrest them."

"Not yet," Rora whispered. She pointed. Down below, in the center of the swarm of chef rats, was Rotten Ruffhouse. He was holding the Big Cheddar and looking at his watch. "Rotten's waiting for someone. It must be the real mastermind. Let's watch to find out who is behind all this."

A moment later, Detective Wolf Growler walked in, and instead of arresting Rotten Ruffhouse, he

shook his hand and smiled. "I see you have the Big Cheddar."

"I do," Rotten said. "Do you remember our orders?"

"I do," Growler said. "We're going to melt this cheese down into fondue and sell it back to the richest of the rich here in Pawston for ten times the price."

"Exactly," Rotten said.

"Gang, I think we've heard enough," Rider said. "Who's ready to stop some bad guys?"

chapter
NINE

PAW! RIGHT IN THE KISSER!

🐾

"Rats, Rotten, Growler, you are all under arrest!" Rider shouted from the skylight above the room. The P.I. Pack swooped down to the factory floor on ropes.

"Oh, rats!" Rotten yelped. "I mean, rats, run for it!"

All the rats with their tiny chef's hats began running around in circles. Rotten made a beeline for the nearest exit. Only Wolf Growler stood his ground.

He scowled at Rider. "You are going to ruin everything! I was supposed to come in and take your place. I would have been known as the best detective in Pawston! I would have had fame and money and all the kibble a dog could ask for!"

"That's not why we work for the law," Rider said. "We do it for truth, justice, and honor! Those are three things you don't have." Rider tackled Growler. The two detectives wrestled and rolled next to the vats of melted cheese.

"Well," Ziggy added, "I do it for the kibble, too."

"Less talk, more action, kid," Rora said as she flipped over an empty basket onto several rats and trapped them.

"I can't believe I finally get to use my Ratcatcher 2000!" Westie said. His invention launched small sticky nets at the whiskered criminals.

Ziggy joined the fight too. He stepped on the tails of two rats.

Then he dipped a piece of bread into the fondue next to him and ate it. "Hmmm. Needs more salt. Where's the head chef?"

Ziggy quickly found the rat ringleader. He was cowering behind the stolen cookbook. "Why'd you do it, chef? I thought *cooks* made good things and *crooks* made bad things?!"

"The Big Cheddar was my final ingredient. I wanted to make the biggest—and tastiest—fondue of all time!" the head chef said. "I would have been famous!"

"So you stole the cheese and the cookbook," Ziggy said. "But why did you steal the CleoCatra arms?"

"Oh, that," the head chef said. "I just don't like cats."

While the P.I. Pack rounded

up the rats, Rider and Growler were still wrestling near the vats of steaming, bubbling cheese. It looked like Growler was winning. "Heel, you old dog," Growler snarled. "I am younger than you, stronger than you, and even smarter than you. Face it, Woofson. I have the upper paw."

"I'll show you what an upper paw looks like," Rider

said. With one quick move, Rider knocked Growler down.

"PAW! Right in the kisser," Rora said. "Nice job, Boss."

"Where'd you learn to fight like that?" Ziggy asked.

"Before I was a detective, I was a boxer," Rider said with a wink. "Trust me, kid. I always have a few tricks up my sleeve."

As the detectives looked over all the rats they'd caught, they realized Rotten had gotten away again.

"I swear that dog has nine lives," Rider said.

"Don't worry," said Rora. "We'll get him next time."

"I'm not worried," Rider said. He walked over to Growler and cuffed him. "Tonight we've brought some cheesy justice back to Pawston instead of letting things go bad. Am I right, 'Detective'?"

Growler whimpered, and Rider smiled.

chapter
TEN

CHEDDAR LUCK NEXT TIME

🐾

The police, the mayor, and the rightful owner of the Big Cheddar were amazed when they arrived at the warehouse.

"Once again, Pawston can't thank you enough, Detective Woofson," the mayor said.

"All in a dog day's work," Rider answered.

"I want to thank you too," said Chip Chipper, the owner of the Chinchilla Cheese Shop. "You and your friends are welcome to free cheese any time."

"Any time?!" Ziggy asked as he reached for the Big Cheddar. "How about now?"

"Ziggy!" cried Rider, Rora, and Westie. "Don't eat the evidence!"

As the police force escorted the rats and the rival detective to jail,

Wolf Growler shook his paw-cuffed fists at Rider. "I'll be back! *Bark* my words! You can't keep a bad dog down!"

With the real culprits arrested, Allie Gator was released. She ran

over to Rider and shook his paw.
"I'm free! You saved me, Detective
Woofson! How can I ever repay
you?"

"With snacks!" Ziggy said.

Rora and Westie rolled their
eyes.

"Really, Ms. Gator, no thanks

needed," Rider said. "Justice is its own reward." The detective looked around at his friends and his admirers. At the beginning of this case, it seemed like the city might not need him anymore, but once again, Rider Woofson had proved that he was one of a kind.

"That no-good, goody-two-shoessss detective ruined my planssss again," Mr. Meow yelled at Rotten Ruffhouse. "How doessss he do it?"

"If you ask me, your plan was kind of *cheesy* anyway," Rotten said, laughing.

Mr. Meow hissed at his hench-dog and dug his claws into a chair.

"I wasssss so closssse. I would have made billionssss from selling that fancy fondue. Plussss Rider would have been replaced by Wolf Growler. And with Growler under

my control, I would have been unsssstoppable. But no, Woofson and his band of bratssss had to ssssave the day. It'ssss not fair!"

"Maybe you'll get him next time," Rotten said with a shrug. Then, under his breath, he added, "If you're lucky."

"I heard that!" Mr. Meow snapped. "Oh, I'm not done yet.

I still have an even bigger crime in store for those "Pee-Yew" Pack stinkerssss. And this plan will be absolutely magical."

Then Mr. Meow threw his head back and cackled with evil delight.

CHECK OUT RIDER WOOFSON'S NEXT CASE!

"Are you kidding me????" Ziggy Fluffenscruff barked. "David Geckom is *the* number one player in the soccer league. He'll totally get voted MVP this year!"

"Kid, I wish you were right, but you don't know what you're talking about," Rora Gooddog said with a laugh. "Lion L. Messy has won it the last two years in a row. Maybe third time's the charm."

Ziggy and Rora were dog detectives and members of the Pup Investigators Pack. They didn't always see eye to eye, but they did have two things in common: They both loved to solve crimes, and they both loved soccer—especially their hometown team, the Pawston Dynamos!

"I've never seen you two this excited about the same thing," Rider Woofson noted. Rider was their boss, and the leader of the

P.I. Pack. "What are you talking about?"

"*Bow-wowza*, Boss! This is only the most important sport in the history of the planet!" Ziggy said, his tail wagging excitedly. "Soccer!"

"This weekend is the big championship match between the Pawston Dynamos and the Catskills Cougars," Rora added. "Ziggy and I both have front-row seats."